Kitty's Place
1860
Lilly Buchanan

Kitty's

Lilly Buchanan

Published by Lilly Buchanan, 2024.

This is a work of fiction. Similarities to real people, places, or events are entirely coincidental.

KITTY'S

First edition. July 9, 2024.

Copyright © 2024 Lilly Buchanan.

ISBN: 979-8227265630

Written by Lilly Buchanan.

To my brother Rob Davis. Thank you for everything. I love you so much! Sister

Dedicated to my brother Rob Davis, I love you! Sister

They had been traveling for 3 months or so, on the journey to cross the dusty country, to go make their fortune. On this one beautiful, windy, evening, they stopped to make camp. Artis went scouting for clean water as his friend set up the area where they would rest. There was a spot up ahead in the distance that looked promising. It appeared to have a few green trees and plants, so Artis rode his horse over to get a closer look. His back was hurting badly, and he hoped the freshwater was there so he could get off of his horse and rest.

It was Luke's idea to ride a world away to go make their fortunes. Luke had met a rich man back in Georgia, where they were from, who swore he struck gold in California, so Luke was determined they would come and make a new life for themselves.

Luke was a brother to him. He would have gone to the moon if that was what Luke wanted to do. He watched Luke suffer so much when his wife was murdered. For absolutely no reason, 2 strangers had just walked into Luke's house and tried to rob his wife Janet, but they had no money. She tried to run for their gun to protect herself but didn't make it, they shot her down, took her wedding band, and then ran away. With the help of the neighbors...Luke and Artis tracked them down, they still had Janet's wedding band. They strung them up and hung them in the town square.

Poor Luke lost the love of his life but was left with his baby girl, Lilly Belle. He couldn't stand the thought of staying in Georgia without his wife. He begged his best friend to go West with him, strike it rich, and live a good life.

His best friend Artis was deep in thought, riding slowly looking for water as Luke set up the camp for the night. They didn't want to camp at a water spot overnight because if there was water, other travelers were sure to follow, and out in the open, you never know who you might happen upon. Criminals or desperate people might steal your property or even kill you for food or money. They had learned to be careful.

Artis rode East for a few minutes when all of a sudden, he realized he heard screaming. He looked over his shoulder and saw horses and Indians where they had stopped to camp. His friend was being attacked by Indians! They were circling the wagon. He rode his horse back as hard and fast as he could to help, firing his rifle as he rode with all his power toward the Indians. However, they left as quickly as they arrived. In a matter of seconds, the attack was over.

His friend, Luke was lying there with 10 arrows stuck inside of him. He lived long enough to beg Artis to care for his daughter Lilly Belle. It can only be described as a miracle that the Indians did not see Lilly Belle, nor that she did not wake up so they could take her with them.

The Indians normally searched the wagons taking what provisions were there, then burned the wagons. Not this time, they killed Luke, took one horse, and then left in a hurry.

"Promise me, Artis. You will raise her as your own. She's only 4 years old. She has no one else. Promise me, brother!" Luke cried.

"I promise friend. I promise." Artis sobbed. Luke had been his best friend since they were little kids.

"I have to go now, there are 2 angels here to take me to heaven. Kiss Lilly Belle for me. Tell her I love her, and I love you brother."

"I will brother. Say hello to my ma and pa if you run into them."

Luke let the air out of his lungs and he was gone. Then there was silence.

Artis dug a grave and buried his friend. Lilly Belle woke up, but Artis asked her to

stay in the wagon so she wouldn't see her father like that. He couldn't get past the

miracle that the Indians did not set the wagon on fire or that the noise they made

did not wake up Lilly Belle. It was truly just a miracle. The Indians were known for that. They hated the white and black men. God knows they had every right to

hate them. Instead of trying to live in peace together, the white people tried to kill

what they did not understand. Artis had witnessed hundreds of burned-up wagons on this trip. He did not understand why God would spare Lilly Belle but he was grateful. He had heard many pitiful mamas recount stories of their children being taken by the Indians. Lilly Belle was a precious little girl. Beautiful blonde hair and green eyes, like her mother, and a fierce determination like her father.

For his best friend to see angels coming to take him to heaven, confirmed what his mama had said all those years ago. Heaven and God were real. He wiped tears from his eyes. No need to let the little girl see him cry, she needed him to protect her and raise her. Artis kept repeating the scenario in his mind. The Indians stole one horse attached to the wagon, but for reasons unknown, they did not take Luke's horse nor ransack the wagon. Lilly Belle was asleep back there. It was a miracle she did not hear the Indians screaming or her father screaming for help and in agonizing pain. Artis kept thinking about this over and over. It was like his mind couldn't comprehend what happened. Yet it was real that Luke was dead.

Artis attached Luke's horse to the wagon, tied his horse behind the wagon and they resumed their journey. Lilly Belle asked for her daddy a few times. Artis kept telling her that her daddy was in heaven with her mama. She didn't understand. What 4-year-old would? Artis tried to teach her to count and to sing a song his mama had taught him. He continued with her nighttime prayers that her daddy had taught her. Artis tried to remember all the games that Luke had played with her.

Thankfully, they didn't come across any more Indians. The journey was easy. Approximately 3 weeks later, they arrived in a boomtown named Moosehead, California. Artis observed the town. It had a mercantile, a hotel, a jail, and a small post office. He rented them a room at the hotel.

Once he put her to bed, he spoke to the hotel manager who recommended one of the more decent, and reliable hotel clerks to watch Lilly Belle. Artis paid her to stay with Lilly Belle in the evenings.

Artis didn't know anything about mining silver or gold but he knew how to talk to people. He knew drinking and women would always be popular with any man. He had put together a business plan, when Lilly Belle was asleep during the journey. He only needed investors to make the dream a reality. Outside a mercantile, while smoking a cigar, Artis found several successful miners who after hearing his proposal agreed to put him in business as a bar and a brothel. They were excited, especially when he promised their return would be threefold. A meeting was held immediately at the hotel, along with a nice dinner and the contracts were drawn up. The men were locals, and they knew all of the contacts for lumber, contractors, plumbing, gas lighting, kitchen and restaurant equipment, beer, and liquor suppliers, and food suppliers. Artis would have to supply the girls.

It took them exactly 2 weeks to work out all of the details and the building began immediately. The saloon and brothel were built in a little over 3 months. There was a saloon downstairs, and 10 rooms upstairs for the working girls. Artis had a kitchen built behind the wall of the saloon.

He also had 2 rooms and a bath built for himself and Lilly Belle, upstairs above the kitchen, away from the working girls.

The builders, three shifts of workers, labored day and night to finish the job. Their motivations were women and liquor. There was a feeling of excitement in the air. The local men stopped in daily to ask about the progress and Artis gladly filled them in.

The men who invested wanted to be silent partners and Artis agreed. They were married, pillars of their small society, and needed to distance themselves. Artis didn't care, he just needed the money to complete the project.

Artis put up signs advertising for working girls. He even paid to have one put on the incoming /outgoing stagecoach that went to different towns to bring back people, packages, and food.

"Looking for 10 beautiful women and 1 ugly one."

The response was overwhelming. 30 ladies applied. He hired 15 of the prettiest and wittiest. He paid for them to stay at the local hotel until his place was ready. He made them sign a promissory note that they would not start working until the saloon was finished. Artis also hired a woman to take care of Lilly Belle full-time while he worked on the new business. The saloon was named Kitty's. Kathreen was Artis' mother's name. Everyone called her Kitty. The bar was very nice, it had a sturdy, brass top, and padded, wood bar stools. It was excellent.

A local craftsman had been contracted to build the tables and chairs that outfitted the inside of the saloon. There were no windows downstairs. Beautiful beds and dressing tables had been built for the upstairs. The rooms were also equipped with dressers, wash areas, and beautiful linen. Artis had 2 of the ladies go into the next town over and find a seamstress who made dresses and lingerie for the working ladies.

A full kitchen was designed by a real chef and his staff. Artis knew they would sell as much food as they did women by the delicious smells that came from that kitchen. Chef Smythe was outstanding and he had an equally wonderful staff.

The grand opening was amazing. Cowboys came from all over to eat, drink and socialize. Artis loved signs. At the door, a sign said, "If you show us your bad side, we will only see it ONCE. Mind yourself."

The self-proclaimed mayor came and had a drink with Artis. His eyes were wide as he marveled at the beautiful ladies. Artis winked at him and told him he could come by any morning before opening and he would introduce him to the ladies. The mayor smiled and winked at him, understanding his meaning. Artis knew it would be smart to have any politicians enjoy his business. You never know when you need a favor. The mayor didn't carry a lot of clout right now, however, as the town grew, he would have connections that could come in handy for any businessman. Artis smiled when he saw the mayor's eyes twinkle.

He would have to keep an eye on him and make sure he didn't visit the girls too much. If his heart gave out while visiting, it would be bad publicity.

Lilly Belle started school at 5 years old. She loved drawing and reading. The school was a lot of fun for her. By the age of 10 Lilly Belle was working in the kitchen of the saloon after school.

Artis repaid his investors, threefold as he promised. He paid them off the first year he was in business, now he was the sole owner.

Kitty's was a huge success. You didn't come to Moosehead without visiting. Even if you just claimed to stop in for steaks and drinks...you had a great time. Word of mouth traveled all over the state of California and visitors came to see for themselves. Artis had a large room built next door to the kitchen for visitors who just wanted to eat and not experience the saloon. He named it Luke's and it stayed busy. When the previous investors saw his success, they tried to talk Artis into going into further business, but he declined. He also hired a local attorney to draw up a will, naming Lilly Belle as his sole heir, and made sure everyone knew she would be the new owner when it was time for him to step down.

One day the teacher heard the older students, mocking and insulting Lilly Belle. "You live in a whore house; my mama told me. She said you probably have diseases, we spose' to stay away from you."

A smaller boy named John Robert pushed the accusers and told them to, "shut up and stop."

Lilly Belle wanted to scream at them and say, "Where do you think your father's come day and night." But she didn't.

She stood there with tears running down her face, letting them insult her. The teacher came running out with a switch and started whipping the other children. "Get inside the schoolhouse right now." She screamed at the top of her lungs.

The injured children limped quickly into the school.

She called the main mocker Bruce Williams to the front of the class. "Bruce, tell us what your father does for a living?'

Bruce hesitated, then looked around the room. He turned bright red. He was embarrassed and wanted to run to the door and escape.

"Tell us!" the teacher screamed.

"He, he don't work." Bruce stuttered.

"Yes, he does. I heard myself, he works as a thief, stealing cattle, goats, chickens anything he can get his hands on."

Bruce hung his head in shame. His face was fire red with embarrassment.

The teacher softened her voice, "Now Bruce. Is that your fault?"

"No, no ma'am I don't have nothing to do with that."

"So, you are the same as Lilly Belle. She is blameless as well. None of us can help

what our parents did or do."

She made each child stand up and tell what their fathers did for a living. It was

humbling. The teacher, Miss Avery, instructed all the children to write a letter to

Lilly Belle and apologize.

"Except you John Robert. I saw you trying to make them stop."

As the last child handed Lilly Belle their letter, it was John Robert, he had drawn a beautiful picture of her.

Lilly Belle smiled at John Robert and mouthed the words, "Thank you"

Lilly Belle asked the teacher if she could tell the class something. The teacher agreed. Lily Belle stood up and began to speak.

"I guess y'all know we came from the south. My daddy wanted to come west and find gold. I was only 4 years old so I don't remember the journey, or my daddy either. I heard it seemed like it took forever in that wagon, but one day when we stopped to rest, the Indians came out of nowhere. That old wagon saved my life because I was sleeping under some blankets. But my daddy, he didn't make it. The Indians shot 10 arrows in him. His best friend Artis was with us on the trip. They grew up together as kids. Artis had gone looking for water, that's why the Indians didn't get him. He came running to help but it was too late, the Indians were gone. Before my daddy died, he made Artis promise he would raise me. He buried my daddy and we went to the next town which was Moosehead. Here he started a business. I help in the kitchen. I am not allowed to go in the front room unless the business is closed. We have 2 rooms upstairs and a bathroom and a living room. It is all away from the business Artis owns. I just wanted to tell you all, that I have no diseases. Artis is a good man, he treats me like his daughter, and that's all I wanted to say."

The class clapped for her and she sat down.

John Robert looked at her with love and admiration. As she had said 10-year-old old Lilly Belle worked in the kitchen after school. She learned under the supervision of a man named Mr. Smythe. He taught her how to cook, wash dishes, and clean the kitchen. She was only allowed in the front of the business when it was closed. She would go in, sweep the floors, and wash the tables with hot water. Artis was always with her when she was in the front room and no customers

were ever allowed in there when she cleaned up.

Occasionally there was gold or coins on the floor under the poker table. Artis let

her keep anything she found, as long as she showed it to him.

Lilly Belle found rings, pocket watches, bullets, gold nuggets, and money. She had

a beautifully decorated box that one of the ladies upstairs had made her to keep her

treasures in. Occasionally the ladies would bring her small pretty things that the

men had given them, for her treasure box.

At the age of 13, Lilly Belle didn't understand why the saloon was so successful. Artis told her, "Men loved to play cards and look at pretty women", so she accepted his explanation. Each week John Robert gave her a beautiful picture. Artis had purchased a notebook for her to keep them in. She wrote on the front of the notebook, Drawings by John Robert.

Then winter came...

The school was out during a long, hard winter, and when spring came they resumed classes. John Robert was not in class. Lilly Belle asked the teacher, "Where is my friend, John Robert?"

The teacher knew that the two were friends, so she called her outside and tried to deliver the message gently.

"I'm so sorry Lilly Belle. John Robert's father pulled him out of school to go work

in the mines. I received word from his father that he would not be coming back."

Lilly Belle cried. She was so upset that the teacher sent her home, to

grieve. She had lost her best friend and did not know if he was ever coming back.

It took several days to come to terms with this loss.

At home, Artis heard her sobs and it broke his heart. He knocked gently on her door, "Lilly Belle, may I come in?"

"Yes sir."

"Miss White says you got upset at school and that your best friend moved away."

Lilly Belle nodded yes. "It just hurts so bad," she said through her tears. "Why did they have to take him? He was a great student in all subjects and you saw how talented he was at art. He was not cut out for manual labor. I just can't believe his daddy has done this. I will miss him so much."

"Well honey, I just want to say I am sorry, and in time it will get better. I know how it feels to lose a best friend." He hugged her and she cried some more. It was 3 days before Lilly Belle was able to go back to school.

Lilly Belle graduated at 16. She had no desire to go to college, nor had she met anyone that she wanted to be her beau. Artis had a serious talk with her, "Sweetie do you know what you want to do in life?"

"I want to stay here and manage the kitchen and the restaurant. Please don't make me go away. I want to stay here with you Artis."

He agreed, hoping she would change her mind.

"It's just that most girls want to get married and have kids. Some girls even go to college. I have money for that." He said.

Lilly Belle laughed and said, "If that day ever comes, I promise to let you know."

He hugged her and said, "Okay."

Lilly Belle learned how to do the market order, the liquor order, hand out payroll, order the beer kegs and manage the employees.

When she turned 18, she was overseeing the working girls, (addressing any concerns they had) and staying with them when they had their medical exams.

The last doctor was taking advantage of them by getting some free sex and the girls hated him, so Lilly made sure the new doctor understood that his payment came from Artis, not the girls.

Lilly Belle had a great rapport with the working ladies. They would have girl talk once a day before the girls began working, so she could find out if there were any issues she needed to address with Artis. Since Lilly Belle was a virgin, she thought what they did was interesting. During one of their girl talks, one of the girls, Santana, had told a curious Lilly Belle that they didn't really have sex for 2 straight hours as the men paid for and that the men mostly cuddled, complained, or professed their undying love. She claimed that some of the younger men were minute men, whose sexual prowess only lasted a minute because they were so excited. Some were so drunk, they passed out once their head hit the pillow and then the girls would wake them, they would tell them how amazing they were in bed for all 2 hours, and last but not least the older men were hands down the best lovers. Lilly Belle was fascinated by this information.

Artis was perplexed. He had limited the girls to 7 drinks a night. They made a nickel from each drink they had, and 75% of the money from each bedding of the customers. However, the girls were getting so drunk, that they were forgetting to count their drinks or collect their pay from the customers.

One day, a foreigner came to the kitchen and asked for Lilly Belle. "Madam, I am Luigi, I have here a product that will change how you make money. It is called wine. It is made from grape juice, sugar, and some other ingredients. I learned to make it in my country, Italy. I am hoping to sell it to you, for your customers and your young ladies."

Lilly Belle called the kitchen staff to gather around to taste it.

"It's very strong," Mr. Smyth said. "But very delicious."

Everyone enjoyed it.

Lilly Belle asked Luigi if he could produce 2 kinds, strong and not strong.

The gentleman said, "Absolutely Madam. I can do that. The longer it ages the stronger it becomes. So, if I sell you young wine, it is not one to get you drunk."

Lilly Belle said, "Great, now I need you to promise not to sell to any other company for a year."

Luigi said, "If you like the wine, I can guarantee you that I will not sell to anyone else for 5 years."

Lilly Belle called over Mr. Smyth for him to shake hands with and seal the deal.

Luigi and the large man shook hands. She figured Luigi might deceive her but not a 6'5, 400lb man.

Lilly Belle purchased the wine from him. That night she sat down with Artis and told him what she had done. As he sampled the wine, she stated, "This way we can serve the girls the one with less alcohol and they can drink all night. They can have 3 real drinks a night and the rest will be the wine that is not strong. Also, we will be accepting payment for the girls before they go upstairs. We just have to write it down and have the girls make their mark by the transaction. If the men want to tip them upstairs, that is fine, and between them.

Artis beamed with pride, "My little Lilly Belle sure has grown up and she has a brain for business! Thank you so much my precious, smart daughter!"

Lilly Belle hugged him, "I wanted to help you. Now the interesting news. We purchased the strong wine. So, we need a night to introduce it to our regulars. We let all of the regulars drink it until their hearts are content for free.

They will be drunk and then miserable for 1 ½ days but then they won't want the wine anymore, and the girls can drink the young wine which is basically fruit juice, from now on."

"We will all lose money that first night" Artis stated, his brow creased with worry.

"Yes, but after that...we will make even more money. The girls can have more customers and more money because they won't be so drunk." Lilly Belle said with a laugh.

Artis was skeptical but he tried to be supportive.

Mr. Luigi arrived, his wine in tow.

They placed the wine bottles in galvanized tubs filled with ice early in the morning. By afternoon it was ready. Artis offered it for free. Every last bit of the

wine was drunk. Those cowboys and miners were drunk beyond belief. By the end

of the night, they didn't even feel like going upstairs for any fun, they just wanted

to throw up and lie down with a cold rag on their heads. Artis was concerned when

he asked Lilly Belle, "Are you sure this will work? We lost a lot of money

tonight, as did the kitchen and the girls."

Lilly Belle giggled and said, "You have my word. If this little experiment was a success, the customers will never want the wine again and the girls will drink the diluted wine and all of us will make more money."

The next day the regulars slowly trickled into the saloon.

They ordered a lot of coffee and food. Every one of them complained of the worst hangover they had ever had. The hardcore card players could not concentrate on their poker games.

Almost all of them complained of headaches, feeling sick to their stomachs, and

feeling dizzy. One of the men threatened to "shoot anyone who went near that piano." Lilly Belle couldn't help but giggle at their misery.

After lunchtime, they ventured into sipping on beer, not whiskey. By the 3rd day, everything was back to normal, except the men did not drink the wine. They ordered their regular beer or whiskey, until about 9 pm, then one by one went upstairs with their favorite girl for 2 hours. That was the maximum time allowed and they paid extra for more time.

Santana told Lilly Belle, "I don't know what was in that drink you call wine, but the next night after it was free no man could have sex, they were all just like a bunch of sick old ladies, who just wanted to be held. It was the damnedest thing I have ever saw."

Lilly Belle laughed and said, "The wine that is coming for you girls to drink is not strong at all. You should be able to drink them men under the table."

"What if they want to taste my wine?" Tiffany asked. Artis laughed heartily and said, "You better tell him you will go and get him a free sample of the wine because he doesn't know where your mouth has been. He will agree with you."

Tiffany was either too hard-hearted or too stupid to be offended by Artis. She just laughed with him.

Within the next 3 days, the business was back to normal. Lilly Belle divided up the wine and cut it with water for the girls. None of the men asked for the wine.

Lilly Belle put a sign in the bathroom that said, "Every man should know his limit." She was being sarcastic after the wine experiment. The sign was right above the sign that said, "Please wash your hands before leaving the bathroom." Which no one ever did.

Doctor Legg came twice a month to check on the girl's health, making sure they

were disease-free and pregnancy-free. Lilly Belle supervised him during the

examinations. This put all the girls at ease.

Samantha came to talk to Lilly Belle early one Friday morning. "I need your help, Lilly Belle. It's about Rasmus. He was a regular customer. About 5'9, 250 lbs., a face only a mother could love, and a bad attitude. He had a crush on Samantha and always paid to go upstairs with her. Samantha had told us he was mean and rough but tipped her good, so she tolerated it. Money was money.

"He hurt me bad last night. I thought he might sleep since he was so liquored up, but he started acting jealous. He started accusing me of loving someone else, and he began punching me, choking me and he forced himself on me, ripping my behind. I can't stop bleeding." Samantha said through her sobs. She opened her coat and her neck was black with his fingerprints where he choked her. Both of her arms were black with bruises, and her legs were bruised and rope marks where he hogtied her and beat her.

Lilly Belle felt sick but told her to go pack her bags. She gathered up some towels to give Samantha to absorb the blood. When Samantha came back, Lilly Belle gave her money to tide her over for 2 months and paid a stagecoach to take her to a hospital 2 towns over.

"Please drive carefully. She is hurt and needs to see the doctor at the hospital." Lilly Belle pleaded with the driver. She gave him a large tip to reinforce her encouragement.

Lilly Belle hugged Samantha and told her, "You can come back in a few months after you heal. I am so sorry this happened to you Samantha under our roof. Just promise to send me a note if you decide not to come back. I will find a way to deal with Rasmus. You are a part of our family." They hugged again and Lilly Belle helped her onto the stagecoach. Samantha was gone.

Lilly Belle walked over to the market. She happened upon some muscled-up men

selling items that were made by a blacksmith. They were new to the area, they

looked rugged.

"How is business gentlemen?" she asked sweetly.

One guy spoke up, "It is very bad. We have been trying to sell this crap for 5 days.

We are out of money, broke, and hungry."

"Lilly Belle said, "I may have a proposition for you."

"We are listening." The 2nd guy said as he stood up, dusted off his hat, and put it back on.

"First, are you planning on staying here, or moving on?"

One of them said, "Ma'am no offense, but we are getting the hell out of this town

as soon as we sell this here junk."

Lilly Belle said, "Well, I run the local saloon, Kitty's. I have a customer who

brutally beat and abused one of my best girls last night. I had to send her away to a

hospital. I will buy all of your inventory, and give you 2 great meals, lunch this

afternoon and dinner tonight, and 2 whiskeys after dinner. I will then point out the

abuser by standing by his table in the saloon and announcing my girl was

brutalized. I want you to teach him a lesson. I am not asking you to kill him, just

humble him. Make sure he knows not to ever come back to this town. Then come

back and let me know you handled it. I don't need details on your ways of persuasion. I will pay you. And you leave town. Can I trust you? Can you accept this offer?"

All 3 men shook her hand and agreed to the task. She gave them money for a bath

and then told them to come for lunch.

After their baths, 2 of them went to the saloon for a meal, and the 3rd stayed to

guard the inventory. As soon as the other 2 ate, they came back and let the 3rd guy

go bathe and then eat. After lunch, they loaded up all of their merchandise and

waited until supper time and delivered it to Lilly Belle's kitchen. Mr. Smyth was

thrilled to have new cast iron kitchenware.

The guys went away for a nap, then came back and had dinner. Cook fed them thick, juicy steaks, fried potatoes, and corn on the cob. Afterward, they went into the saloon and had a few drinks at the bar.

As planned, when Rasmus came in, Lilly Belle let him have one whiskey, then she

went and stood by him. The 3 men were not surprised when she stood by the big,

ugly coward who could probably beat up any woman in the brothel.

Lille Belle announced, "Everyone may I have your attention please. I am sorry, but

Samantha won't be with us tonight. Some piece of dog crap beat her half to death

last night. She is unable to work tonight or maybe never again."

Lilly Belle then stepped away from Rasmus and went to the kitchen.

One of the guys walked over to Rasmus and said, "Can you help me out, partner?

My horse is looking puny and I need a second opinion on him."

Rasmus grunted and said, "I ain't no damn horse doctor."

The other 2 men walked over to the table. One of the men pushed up his vest to show his gun that was in his pants.

"This ain't no request you ole bastard curly wolf. Come outside now."

Rasmus pushed away from the table and walked towards the saloon doors.

He hit the doors hard and tried to make a run for it, but was hit in the head from

behind, and fell face down in the dirt. It knocked him out. The 3 men picked him

up, and put him across his horse, and rode him out of town. Once out of the town

sightline, they pulled him down and hog-tied him like he did Samantha. He was

just coming to, and asked, "What the hell?" One of the men grabbed Rasmus by his

hair held up his head, and said, "You a real tough guy. Beating up whores and taking away their way of making money. That don't go around here. And that nice

lady that owns that saloon you broke her heart. Nope, we don't put up with that.

Say adios boy."

He dropped Rasmus's head back down hard, and they dragged him for miles back

and forth across the rugged terrain until they were sure he was dead. They dug a

deep hole and put what was left of him in that hole.

They went back to the restaurant to meet with Lilly Belle.

They were smiling at Lille Belle as she approached them at the kitchen door. She

held up her hand and said, "I don't want to know. But I do want you to know I am

grateful." She handed them each an envelope and kissed them each on the cheek.

The men looked shocked, each man was embarrassed and mumbled that she was welcome.

"Just let me say, ma'am, he said he won't be coming back here."

She said, "Thank you" again.

They rode away and she never saw them again.

Some things can't be handled with conversation. Some men only understand action.

4 months later, Lilly Belle received a letter from Samantha. She met a doctor named Avery Johanson, and they are engaged to be married. She said she was healing nicely and was safe and in a good place. The doctor had his own home, with servants and they were to have a real church wedding. His mother was very kind to her and was thrilled to have her as a soon-to-be daughter-in-law. Samantha said that because of her attack, she would never be able to have children and Avery was aware of this and has agreed to adopt whenever she feels she is ready. A nanny or 2 would be provided to her to help with the children. Like a dream come true. Samantha thanked Lilly Belle for everything she had ever done for her and told her she loved her. I will write to you again and send you pictures

of my wedding." I know you will be happy for me. I love and miss you. Samantha."

Lilly Belle hated to lose Samantha, but she completely understood Samantha needed a new life. Rasmus nearly killed the poor girl and death can make you reprioritize your goals in life. Lilly Belle found herself smiling, happy for Samantha, and wishing the same happiness for all of the ladies who worked in the saloon. She put the letter in her private lock box and decided not to tell Artis. He would have been upset. Samantha had been a favorite. Lilly Belle would advertise for another beautiful girl to take Samantha's place. The good people of Moosehead were very protective of Kitty's. The attraction to Kitty's brought a lot of foot traffic to the area.

If strangers came to town and started any trouble in the saloon, the regular customers would handle any situation without being asked. One night, a Spanish guy, who came in drunk, grabbed the waitress and tried to force himself on her in front of everyone. Two cowboys, Mitchell and Johnny, at the bar pulled the waitress away from him quickly, drug the guy outside, and gave him a whopping. Then they tied him to a pole until he sobered up. He was never allowed in Kitty's again. That didn't stop him from trying to come in but he never got past the security at the saloon doors.

For the majority of men, Kitty's was a place of refuge, and they would not stand for any violence to the women, tearing up the place or disrespecting any of the staff, especially Lilly Belle or Artis. Not that some rogues hadn't tried to push their way around. For the most part, a large percentage of the men were decent. There were often times that poker players would cause a scene. Artis knew who the high rollers were and he knew who was green and didn't know an Ace from a Jack.

Artis would pull the high rollers aside and tell them. "I run a clean joint here. We don't cheat anybody. I will be glad to set you up a table outside and y'all can play all you want but no high stakes in Kitty's. So, what's it gonna be?" Each time the high roller would say, I will just take my business elsewhere!" and Artis would say, "Yes you will. Kitty's makes its money off of food, whiskey, and tail. Not confidence games and trickery. Anything a man buys in my place knows exactly what he is getting. I am not against a harmless game of cards. But see your reputation proceeds you sir, and you have a habit of shooting people who beat you and you will not do it here. Everyone knows I run a nice clean place. Now shall you leave quietly or will my staff show you the exit?" The card shark usually left quietly.

The patrons of Kitty's admired Artis for his honesty and standards. He was like everyone's big brother.

Artis was wiping down the bottles and getting the saloon ready to open, it was almost time. Mr. Smythe came in from the kitchen and said, "Boss, there is a lady to see you."

Artis said, "Send her in."

Mr. Smythe escorted the lady in.

Artis felt his face flush red and he couldn't speak for a minute. The lady was

absolutely the prettiest thing he had ever seen. She had long curly brown hair,

brown eyes, a tiny waist, a long neck, large breasts, and gorgeous legs.

She smiled when she saw his reaction.

"Hello, sir. My name is Rachel Blackstock. I would like to apply for the position

you have open in your saloon."

Artis took her hand and kissed it.

"I am, I am, Artis, I am Artis, the um, the owner. Forgive me. You are stunning."

Rachel smiled and said, "Thank you very much for your kind words."

Artis regained his senses, "My daughter must have put out an advertisement. We lost a young lady several months ago. She was very sweet. I hate that she left. Can

you tell me about yourself? Pardon my manners...would you like something to drink? We have coffee, tea, or something stronger?"

Rachel smiled and said, "Coffee will be nice. Cream and sugar if you don't mind."

"No problem at all young lady."

He darted into the kitchen and came back with her coffee and a sweet roll. Lilly

Belle came in and he asked her to open the saloon while he spoke to Rachel in the

restaurant.

They moved their conversation to the restaurant. Lilly Belle smiled because she

had never seen Artis smitten with a woman and smitten was written all over his

face.

Rachel and Artis talked for hours. Meanwhile, 2 other ladies came in to talk to

Lilly Belle about the position available in the brothel. They were more suitable and

she told them she would have an answer for them the next day. Artis bought Rachel

dinner at the Hotel across the street and took her on a buggy ride. She was funny,

she laughed at his jokes, and he just kept falling. When she spoke about her past,

she looked sad. "My parents were dirt poor. The government took all of their

children away. I had one little brother and 7 sisters. They put us in different institutions or orphanages so we could not see each other. When I turned 16, I was

told to get out. I had been abused by most of the men workers, so being thrown out

was a blessing to me. I am now 25 years old. I have waitressed, cleaned houses,

worked on a farm, and done all types of jobs to feed myself, and to keep a roof

over my head. I have no formal education.

Artis just adored this young woman. "Rachel, have you ever thought of getting

married?"

Rachel smiled and said, "Who would marry me, sir? The orphanage made sure I

was damaged goods. I am 25 years old. No decent man would want me."

Artis took her hand and said, "Listen Rachel. I know we just met, but how about

we get to know each other? Every person in this town can vouch for me that I am a

good decent man. I do not sleep with the girls who work for me. I do not date any

of them. They are like family to me. Maybe I am the man for you. I have never

been married. I never found the woman who made me feel the way that you do. I

felt like lightning hit me when you walked in. You would have a home, a safe place

to live, I would protect you. No one would ever hurt you again, I would make sure

of that. I don't want to see other men touching you or know they are having sex with you.

I want to marry you and we make love to each other. I can afford for us to have a good life."

Rachel began to cry real tears. No man had ever made that offer to her. She smiled

and said, "Okay, let's give it just a little time and make sure this is what you want."

He hugged her and said, "Oh my goodness. Yes! Let's get to know each other and

see if we can make this work. I will never use your past against you. I swear."

Artis went to the hotel desk and paid for one month for a suite for Rachel.

He sent a porter to pick up her bags at his restaurant. She had left them near the

kitchen door. He also told the manager to run a tab for anything she needed,

toiletries, meals, baths...anything. And he would pay for it."

Once Rachel got settled in her room, she cried happy tears. She began to pray and

thank God for smiling on her again. Artis had the clerk send for a seamstress to fit

Rachel for new dresses and he sent for the jeweler so he could pick out a ring for

her. He wanted all of the world to know she was spoken for.

Lilly Belle worked hard that afternoon into the evening. Artis finally came back

without the beautiful woman she saw him with earlier in the day.

"Okay Pops, spill the beans, who is she?"

Artis smiled and said, "Hopefully the woman I will marry. Her name is Rachel

Blackstock."

Lilly Belle looked shocked.

Artis laughed, "Initially she came here for a job, apparently you have advertised

for more ladies, but honey she isn't a working girl."

"Well, it's a good thing I hired those other 2 girls this afternoon. I can't count on

you to do the hiring." Lilly Belle said with a giggle.

"I might let her work in the kitchen if she wants to. I haven't asked her yet. Oh,

Lilly Belle, she is so sweet. I am crazy about her." Artis gushed.

"I'm glad you are so happy Dad. You deserve to be happy."

Artis blushed. "You know of all the women we have had come through here, none

of them have caught my attention like her. She makes me want to settle down, raise

some cattle, grow some vegetables, sit down at a table, and eat dinner with her

every night."

"That's amazing Dad. What does she want?"

"Honestly honey, I think she wants what all women want. To be loved."

A man who came to Moosehead, to make his fortune in the mines and failed miserably. He had bought a mine from a crooked man and the mine was bare. He had been tricked. His name was Bart, short for Barthelme. He was a big man, over 6 feet tall. He had rich red hair, shoulder length, and a massive beard. He was a handsome man but a look of despair was in his eyes. He approached Artis for a job.

"The mines have let me down. I've lost everything." He said softly, as they stood outside the back door of the restaurant. "I've sold everything just to eat. I ain't even got a horse."

Artis told Mr. Smythe to fix them a steak and all the fixings.

"Sir, I can't pay you. I just told you I'm busted." Bart said with tears in his eyes.

Artis said, "Let's eat first, then talk business."

They ate and drank a few beers. Bart was very grateful for the meal. It had been

several days since he had eaten anything. His last meal had just been beans. His

stomach was grateful for the food.

Artis asked Bart to tell him about his life before Moosehead.

"Well sir, I lived in North Carolina. I was a farmer, quite a successful farmer. I was

engaged to be married to a nice lady. Her name was Angela. My brother and I

were building a house for my bride-to-be, and me to live in. Life was very good.

Then in the middle of one night, her father came beating on my door demanding to see her. I told him she wasn't there, that she and her mother had come by in the daytime to get some vegetables but that was in the daytime.

He started to cry and said they never came home. I woke up my brother, we got

dressed and went searching for them.

We found their wagon the next morning in a cornfield.

Her mother's dead body was there, but my beautiful Angela was not there.

We never did find her. After 2 years of searching, I gave up and moved out here to

mine for gold. I couldn't stand being there without her."

"I am so sorry Bart. That is a terrible situation. I can't imagine not knowing."

"Yes sir, that is the hardest part. But I'm ready to start over. The mining thing didn't work out, so I'm ready to work for you. I am an honest man. You can trust

me. My word is good."

"I'm glad to hear that Bart! I'm having some small houses built, 25 of them, and I

need an overseer for the rental properties. On the rentals, I would need you to rent

the houses, collect the rent every month, and repair anything that needs fixing,

unfortunately, sometimes you will have to put people out who don't pay. That will

be difficult but you have to explain to them when they sign the contracts, business

is business. So if they do not pay they cannot live in the house.

I will also have some houses for sale for the successful minors. The buyers will pay

money to purchase those homes. It will be difficult but I am in business to make

money. I also need you to be my eyes and ears. I will also have some houses for

sale for the successful minors. The buyers will pay money to purchase those

homes.

I also intend to have some of the renter's farm vegetables for me to use in the

restaurant. I will adjust their rent accordingly. Is this something you would be

interested in? I will pay you handsomely."

Bart's eyes watered up. "I am so honored that you think enough of me to offer me

this job. Yes, I will gladly accept."

Artis smiled and said, "I know you are a good man, Bart. I am also giving you a house to live in. You can eat here until you get your first pay. I think this will be a great adventure. I found out about this kind of way of doing business when I went to purchase supplies in Maresville, a few towns over. A group of men were discussing building houses and I heard it all. I have the money to take on this project and I know I can trust you to help me."

"I think it is a great idea, Artis. Thank you so much for hiring me. I won't let you

down. I promise. I am an honest man. I will work hard for you sir."

Artis smiled and said, "I believe you, Bart. I'm also going to build a boarding

house for miners. The hotel will be mad for a bit, but it will keep the miners closer

to their claims. It will be temporary housing but I want you to focus on the family

homes. Until you get acquainted with them, I don't want to overload you."

"Yes sir, I understand." The gentle giant answered.

After lunch, they rode out to the neighborhood where the houses were being built.

Bart was extremely impressed. The houses were nice, with shutters on the

windows, front porches, and clotheslines. He could imagine bed sheets blowing in

the wind on laundry days.

Artis pointed out, "There will be a neighborhood store that sells groceries, home supplies, and animal feed over there."

Bart whistled and said, "All of that in one store? You have thought of everything

Artis. This is a great idea and it will be a wonderful opportunity."

Artis said, "Thanks. As the houses fill up, you can hire a man to help you with

maintenance and a woman to help with the books. There is room for growth. The

town is growing so people can get jobs and not just depend on the mines to give

them money. They have to be positive and think of ways to survive. You may have

to put these ideas in their heads. Maybe sell some of their fruits and vegetables to

the surrounding stores or people in the area? Help with farm chores? There are so

many ways to make extra money. Your maintenance man will have to clean the

houses as soon as they are vacant so we can have a quick turnover, meaning rent

them or sell them as soon as they are available."

Bart nodded his head and said, "Yes sir."

Artis took Bart to his new home. It was huge, 2 bedrooms, a kitchen with a wood

burning stove, a living room with a fireplace, a dining room, and a fireplace that

connected the 2 bedrooms It was already partially furnished with a bed, a desk and

chair, 2 chairs for the living room, 2 lamps, linen, and rugs.

"Lilly Belle furnished this home for whomever I decided to hire...which is you,

Bart. Please remember, I chose you because you are an honest man.

I will take care of you financially as you protect what is mine."

Bart teared up and said, "Sir, I just don't have the words, except, Thank you from the bottom of my heart."

They shook hands and the deal was made.

"I am having some signs made up that will say, 'Houses for rent or sale. See Bart. In front of your house, a sign will say, Manager: Bart

People know me in this town, and they know I am a no-nonsense type of man. If I

make any deals with the men, I will introduce you to them and explain they are to

pay you every month, because you are my manager. I will also make it clear to the

men that if they do not pay on time, they will have 15 days to move out. There are

going to be times you have to enforce this. I have learned there are different kinds

of people in the world, some are givers and some are takers. The takers will take all

you let them carry, so we have to be smart."

Bart nodded his head to say he understood.

Artis smiled and said, "I know you are new to this but you will catch on very

quickly. If you listen to me, I will make both of us some money.

I have put up signs in the towns to the east of us and the north of us, advertising

houses for rent and sale. I am figuring on a lot of families moving to the area in a

short time. As you see the builders are working hard to make those houses ready to

live in. I think it is just the thing this town needs.

Sleeping in tents can't be good for a man or woman's back."

"I can vouch for that sir. I could never get comfortable. I can't wait to sleep in a

bed again." Bart said with a big smile on his face.

Artis looked at him and said, "Bart. Say, I was wondering, is there anything specific you want?"

"Well, I always wanted to get married and have a family. Maybe one day I will.

And I always wanted to have a horse farm."

Artis chuckled and said," Well, I can't get you a bride, but when you are ready, I

can help with the horses." Artis stopped the carriage at McDaniel's Horse and

Tackle, and let Bart pick out 3 horses. They also purchased the saddles and the tacts.

Artis smiled as Bart said, "Oh my goodness! Thank you so much! I guess I have to

get the bride myself. But I don't want any of those women they bring in on the

stagecoach who have never met their new husbands. I want to meet a nice woman

and court her, I guess I'm old-fashioned."

"Aint nothing wrong with that Bart. I always heard the good Lord provides. Now

you go and meet up with Lilly Belle to get the list for your new house and we will

start work in the morning around 9 am. Okay?"

"Yes sir, sounds great. Oh, my goodness. I'm off to a great start with a wonderful

job and a horse farm. Thank you again so much sir."

"My pleasure. I got a good feeling about this."

They shook hands, but Bart couldn't help but hug Artis.

Bart couldn't believe how things had turned around for him. One day homeless and

a failure as a gold miner, then next a manager of houses, working for the most

successful man in Moosehead and owning 3 of his own horses. He could almost hear his grandmother saying, "What a difference a day makes." She used to say

that to cheer him up when he was disappointed as a child.

He rode back to the house, leading the 3 horses to the barn, and was in shock at

how nice the house was. There was a barn for his horse, 2 acres for a garden, and

room for flower beds. A corral for the horses and land for them to run on.

The house he and his brother were building couldn't hold a candle to this place.

There were curtains and a table, the bed was amazing with 2 pillows, sheets, and a

bedspread. There were towels and washcloths, the fireplace and wood in it ready to

use, the stove had wood near it ready to use.

There was a well outside, with an outhouse, and upon further inspection, there was

an outside shower. Bart was so happy. Looking inside his home he spotted a Bible.

He hadn't opened a Bible since Angel had disappeared. He sat down in the chair

and opened the Bible. It opened to Psalms 107:1-3 (Oh give thanks to the Lord, for

He is good, for his mercy endureth forever.) Bart had been mad at God for 2 years

for not letting him find Angel.

He had not stepped foot inside a church, opened a bible, or prayed but today

seemed to be a new chapter in Bart's life, and he was grateful. He prayed and

thanked God for turning his life around.

"Hello Lord. It's me, Bart. I know it's been a long time since I called on you. I

don't need a thing. I just wanted to say thank you for turning things around for me.

I never stopped believing in you. I was just angry that you allowed someone to

take Angel from me. I was hurt and I felt like maybe I wasn't good enough for her

and that's why you let someone else have her, you see I never thought she was

dead like her mama. I always thought someone just took her. Someone with money

who could give her a better life than me. I was always scared I would find her and

she wouldn't want to come back because I was poor and she now had a better life.

It was easier to think that way than to think someone had taken her and killed her. I

still don't have an answer to that, but I pray wherever she ends up at that she is

happy and is living a good life. I'm sorry I was so mad at you Lord. You have been

good to me even when I don't deserve it. Thank you for forgiveness, thank you for

your mercy. Help me Lord to be the best man I can be. Please bless Artis for

showing me favor and giving me this job and this house. I am so thankful. Lord

show me how to do a good job. Lead me in your ways Lord.

Amen.

Bart went out to the barn and fed and watered his horses. He was so thrilled to watch them. They were so beautiful. He heard a carriage pulling up and turned to

see Lilly Belle arriving. He walked out to greet her.

"I was coming to see you in a little bit." He said as he waved.

"I thought I would save you the ride. I know my daddy has had you out most of the

day." Lilly Belle said with a chuckle.

Her wagon was loaded down with things. She had dishes, cups, a coffee pot,

cooking pots, baking dishes, eating utensils, cooking utensils, curtains, curtain

rods, tools (hammer, screwdriver, nails, screws, tape, hand saw) kitchen towels to

dry dishes with, basin to wash dishes in, logs for the fireplaces and wood burning

stove, bath towels and soap, an extra set of sheets and a comforter for the guest

bedroom, a tea pitcher, and groceries.

"Oh my goodness Lilly Belle you shouldn't have done all this," Bart said.

Lilly Belle smiled and said, "You are our manager and we want you to be happy at

home. Now we still want you to come and eat lunch and dinner at the restaurant

until you get your first check. I didn't know if you knew how to cook or not so I

brought easy stuff to prepare."

"Well, to be honest, I am not the best cook."

"That's okay. Mr. Smyth loves to teach folks how to cook. On Saturdays, he can

teach you and you will enjoy it.

I'm telling you by the 4th Saturday you will have the confidence of a restaurant

chef."

"Well sign me up then!" Bart said in a cheerful tone.

Together they unpacked the carriage. He rode his horse next to her carriage to

escort her back to Kitty's.

"I'm so happy daddy picked you Bart as a manager. I think you are a great fit. He

needs someone he can depend on to do the right thing. He is pretty busy with the

saloon and the restaurant."

Bart smiled and said, "Lilly Belle, I am so happy he picked me. I needed this so

badly. I'm going to do a good job for him."

Lilly Belle smiled and said, "I believe you will Bart. I really do. Oh, there is one

more thing I need to give you when we get to Kitty's."

Bart said, "Okay."

They talked along the way, so time flew by. She reloaded the wagon with a few more things. As he was leaving, she met him outside and handed him a shotgun and some shotgun shells, a pistol, and some bullets.

"I pray you never need to use these, but some folks around here only speak this

language so protect yourself, Bart."

He shook his head yes and said, "Yes ma'am. Thank you."

"You are welcome. Take the rest of these things home then come back for dinner."

Bart tipped his hat and thanked Lilly Belle. He went home and cleaned up as best he could, that shower was cold but it felt great. He headed back to Luke's restaurant. On the way there, he met a man on the same path. The rider only had one arm; however, he was very proficient with his riding and had great manners. They struck up a conversation.

The gentleman spoke first, " JR sir, nice to meet you."

"I'm Bart, where ya headed?"

"Hopefully to get a good meal." The stranger answered as he chuckled.

"You better follow me then mister. Luke's restaurant has the best of anything you want to eat. By the way, I promise you."

The stranger said, "Nice to hear. I'm starving."

After that they didn't carry on a conversation, they just rode in silence.

They arrived at Luke's and it was extremely busy.

"Is it always this packed?" Luke asked.

"Yes, the food is unbelievable, folks come from all over." Bart answered

The waitress got them a table, and 2 beers and took their orders.

"So, what do you do for work Bart?"

"I am the new manager of houses for Mr. Artis. He and his daughter own this saloon and restaurant. He rents houses and sells houses. I will collect rents and sales money. Tomorrow is my first day, but I am excited."

The men ate, and Robert insisted on paying for dinner. They went around the building and went into the saloon. Artis got them 2 beers and they sat over to the side. Bart did most of the talking about how excited he was about his new job. Artis joined them and Robert asked, "Sir, is Miss Lilly Belle here?"

Artis laughed and said, "Well now, that depends, what do you want with her?"

Robert smiled and pointed at a pencil drawing of Lilly Belle up on the wall. "You see that beautiful picture of a gorgeous, 10-year-old girl? I sir, am the artist that drew that. I am John Robert."

Artis's mouth fell open. "Don't you move I will get her." He yelled into the kitchen, "Somebody get Lilly Belle, it's important. I need her."

Bart excused himself and left through the kitchen. He felt like this was a private moment that he wasn't needed in. He was right.

Lilly Belle came running into the saloon to see what her dad needed. He had never called for her like that so she was sure something was wrong. He motioned for her to come around to the other side of the bar. There stood John Robert. At first, she froze, then she rushed to him. They hugged, then both began to cry.

Lilly Belle said, "I can't believe it is you after all this time. I've missed you so much, John Robert."

"I've missed you too honey." He said, wiping the tears from her face with his handkerchief. Lilly Belle sat down next to him. She turned to Artis and said, "Dad, this is my friend from school. This is my best friend who had to leave school." They shook hands.

"It's very nice to meet you, son," Artis said with a smile.

"Tell me about your life," Lilly Belle begged.

"I worked in my daddy's mine but I wasn't very good at it. At 15, I became a

supervisor. I was excellent at drawing maps and skilled at ways to build the shafts.

When I turned 18, we had a cave in and I went in to help rescue our crew. The

shaft gave way and I lost my left arm when I was buried under some rocks. I was

lucky. I got out with my life. We lost 5 men that day. It was a terrible, terrible

situation. We closed down the 3 mines that we had and my daddy opened a 4th

mine. It was there we made our fortune. It was filled with gold. He was so excited

that his heart gave away before he could enjoy one ounce of the gold."

"Oh, John Robert. I am so sorry. But I am so happy to see you. I have missed you every day since you left me. You didn't even get to say goodbye."

"Lilly Belle, are you married?" John Robert asked.

She smiled and said, "Not even close to being married. I work a lot and I don't date

anyone. You?"

He smiled and said, "No, not even close until today. Do you know of anyone that

could love a one-armed man?"

Lilly Belle said, "Shoot, I know a girl who has always loved a man whether he had

one arm or no arms."

Artis watched them and tears fell from his eyes. He was so excited for his

daughter; he wanted her to be happy. John Robert asked Lilly Belle to marry him

right there in the bar.

"We can rent one of your Daddy's houses until we can have

one built. Lilly Belle was so happy, that she cried. "Yes, that will be wonderful."

Artis reminded her that she had to watch the bar so he could go get Rachel and

bring her over for dinner. Lilly Belle told him to hurry and go get her so they could

get to know her too.

As Artis ran out, Lilly Belle explained how the business worked, "John Robert,

you have to understand, this is a family-run business. Yes, we have whiskey,

women, and gambling. I mainly work with the restaurant and the kitchen.

I do however, supervise the girls upstairs when the doctor comes to check on them so they don't get taken advantage of, but we have got a good reputation. We don't

hire thieves. If one gets past us, we run them off. The girls are paid handsomely,

and we make a good living too. My dad doesn't allow big-time gamblers in here,

only friendly games. It cuts down on the shooting and killing that comes with the

high stakes."

John Robert looked at her and then kissed her hand. "Will you still work when our

babies come?"

Lilly Belle looked surprised and said, "I hadn't thought of that. I guess I will take

over the real estate part of the business when that happens. Or maybe even open

another business away from my dad altogether. I guess we need to talk about that

honey. I feel like he may want to hire managers when he marries.

He is crazy about this lady Rachel. I guess we will have to see how it works out.

Do you want to work right now?"

John Robert smiled and said, "I want to work a ranch, a farm, and take care of a

bunch of kids with my lovely wife. We are financially secure for the rest of our

lives. I want to spend my time making you happy and being happy with you."

Lilly Belle teared up again. "I can't believe you are here. It is like a dream come

true for me. I thought I was going to be working here the rest of my life and never have a family of my own. I never saw it happening for my dad either. Life is funny,

isn't it?"

John Robert grabbed her hand. "I want you to know, that I intend to propose to you

again, in a more romantic setting Lilly Belle. I just could not contain myself when I

saw you. I can't let myself be parted from you again."

"You won't have to dear. I am yours. I have always been yours."

"We can have a big wedding and invite everyone that you want." Lilly Belle

smiled big and said, "It would be wonderful even if were just the two of us."

———————————

Artis and his new sweetheart Rachel came back from the hotel and had dinner in

the restaurant. They talked for hours. Rachel had a beautiful radiant look of love

upon her face and Artis was smitten with her. They were falling in love.

Rachel cried and Artis held her. He walked her back to the hotel and kissed her

goodnight. He floated back to Kitty's and relieved Lilly Belle from behind the bar.

The crowd was large and everyone was having a great time.

John Robert and Lilly Belle left the bar and went for a carriage ride. Lilly Belle

showed him the housing development that her dad was having built. John Robert

was very impressed however, he said, "Honey, this is beautiful but I want to show you some plans I have been working on for years. We can make any changes you

desire, but I believe you will love it when you see the design. It is pretty

phenomenal if I do say so myself."

Lilly Belle smiled big and, "Sweetheart, I am sure the house is going to be

amazing."

"Well, it is for an amazing woman, my soon-to-be wife." John Robert said with a smile.

"Aww thank you, honey. Dad will help us find the perfect land to build on." Lilly

Belle said. "I think he and I need to have a conversation about hiring a couple more

managers for the business. We need more downtime now that we are courting and

being courted."

"That is strictly up to you two."

That evening when John Robert dropped Lilly Belle back off at Luke's restaurant,

he went over to the Hotel and rented a room for the night. He was so excited he

could barely sleep. He tossed and turned, finally, he sat up and began to pray. He

thanked God for allowing him to find Lilly Belle still single and willing to love

him even though he had just one arm. When he finished praying, John Robert felt

calmer. He laid back down and was able to go to sleep.

Back at Kitty's, when Artis was closing up, Lillie Belle came in to help clean up the saloon.

"Sweetie, what are you doing up so early?" Artis asked.

"Haven't been to sleep, Dad." She said with a smile.

"Yeah, we have a lot going on right now don't we?"

"Yes sir. I know you don't want to sell Dad, so we need to think about hiring some

on-site managers to run things if we are going to have any kind of lives outside of

here. Mr. Smythe is perfectly capable of running the kitchen as a manager. But we

need a bar manager, a manager for the girls upstairs, and a restaurant manager.

John Robert is talking about marriage, a home, and children. I can't do this and that

too Daddy."

Artis walked over and hugged her.

"I know honey. I would not expect you to. I want to give Rachel a normal life too.

I asked her if she wanted to run the restaurant until I could hire a manager and she

said yes that would be fine, but I would only want her to do it while I was working

during the day. I still don't know how I feel about that."

Lilly Belle said, "Well, we have some options, for the bar and the restaurant we can

put some advertisements in the papers in surrounding cities asking for experienced

managers, they must have excellent references that we can contact and meet with

to verify their legitimacy.

Or I can travel to different cities to meet one-on-one with different applicants as a surprise meeting at their jobs to see how they operate.

As far as the girls, we can promote one of the girls upstairs to manage over the

other girls to see how that goes. Give her a fat salary and some responsibility and

see if she abuses it. Let her know if she messes up, she is fired with no references.

Make her keep a journal of her duties and expenses. I can train the one we pick.

There are only 3, I would pick to become a manager."

Artis looks at her and smiles, "Baby, you have truly put some thought into this. I could still have a hand in helping Bart with the real estate side of it. That would be enough to keep me out of Rachel's hair all of the time."

Lilly Belle laughed and said, "Oh my goodness, I forgot about that! Yes, it would."

It had been about 6 months since John Robert arrived. He was ready to be married and spend the rest of his life with Lilly Belle. Artis too was growing impatient.

Artis and John Robert searched for months for the perfect acreage to build Lilly Belle's house. They finally found it a few miles outside of Moosehead. There were rolling hills for the cattle and horses, a perfect area for the vegetable garden and flower gardens, the barns, and of course the house. The two men had become very close in the last couple of months and already felt to be family.

When the two men arrived back at Kitty's, Lilly Belle and Mr. Smythe were interviewing men for the saloon manager position. 10 men had arrived for interviews. Artis and John Robert both could tell by the look on Lilly Belle's face that she was not impressed with any of them.

"Dad, I gave each of them fare to get them back to where they came from. I have never in my life met such arrogant, hateful, men in my life. Two of them came right out and said they don't take instructions from no woman. I did not even bother to tell them you were the owner. Plus all of them agreed that high-stakes poker would be allowed if they were hired because that is where all the good money is at and the girls upstairs should only be making 30% of their take. I wanted to shoot all of them on the spot."

Mr. Smythe just grunted and shook his head in disgust.

Artis hugged her and said, "Calm down daughter. They are all gone now. You handled it just as I would, except for giving them fare home." He laughed. John Robert did not like to see her upset but he knew it would be difficult to hire people they could trust to take care of the businesses.

John Robert said, "Sweetheart, it sounds like you asked all the right questions, it is just that all the wrong men came to interview. Maybe you should alter your advertisement to include no cads, no arshwholes."

Artis and Lilly Belle both laughed and the mood lightened. Lille Belle hugged John Robert and said, "I just might have to do that babe."

Bart was having amazing success with renting the houses in the real estate division. He was a great manager. Everyone was paying their rent or mortgage on time, and people were growing their gardens in preparation for using some of their produce to take off the rent. There was only one incident where a frustrated miner beat up his wife badly, and Bart handled it by beating him badly. He had been a model husband after that incident.

Many men had sent for their families to join them, and the town was growing by leaps and bounds. Several of the men had struck gold and silver in their mines and decided to stay on in Moosehead, raise their children, and start businesses.

Artis was very proud of Bart. He gave him a raise, and 3 more horses, invited him to all family functions, and he met a lady he wanted to introduce him to. He had met her while he and Rachel were meeting with an architect in the next town. She was the secretary of the company. Rachel had struck up a conversation with her. Her name was Candish.

Candish was 19. She had come from Alabama with her parents and her little brother. Her father wanted to make his fortune. They were robbed of all their worldly goods as soon as they arrived outside of Kingerton.

Her father stood up to the outlaws. They shot him and her mother in the head, killing them both instantly. They ordered Candish and her little brother out of the wagon and stole the wagon. A man on the way to Kingerton came along in a wagon and picked them up and sent someone to bury their parents. One of the architects and his wife took them in and gave her a job there at the firm as a secretary. She was a very sweet girl.

Timothy the architect spoke highly of Candish and Randy her little brother. He also stated they had just found out his wife was expecting their first child so they were going to help Candish get her own home.

Artis asked him if he could invite Candish and Randy to spend some time with them and see if they like Moosehead. He told him about Bart. The architect was thrilled. "I will discuss it with Candish and will send them on a carriage next Monday if she agrees. I will send you a post tomorrow to let you know if she agrees. However, I do not foresee a problem at all."

Artis and Rachel were thrilled. Once they were back in Moosehead, they sent Bart word to get one of the houses ready, just telling him it was for some important guest. Rachel furnished it. Bart had been so good to them. They wanted to do something special for him. He had been honest with Artis when he told him he wanted a wife and a family.

The post came the next day stating that Candish and her brother would be arriving the next week with all their belongings. The architect stated she was excited about the new start. Her brother Randy was 4 years old and was happy under any circumstances as long as he was with Candish.

Rachel had made sure he had plenty of toys to play with in his room. Artis even provided him with a pony. Everyone was excited for their arrival. Only Bart was in the dark.

Artis asked Bart to clean up good to help him meet the visitors who were coming in the next day on the carriage at noon. Bart was curious but he just said, " yes sir."

The next day, the carriage arrived as scheduled. As the dust settled, Bart waited to open the door and a small hand reached out. It was Randy. Bart reached around his waist and helped him down. Bart said, "Well hello partner."

Randy smiled and said, "Hello. I'm Randy. I'm 4."

The next hand that came out belonged to Candish. Just touching her hand made Bart's heart race. She stepped out and she was gorgeous. Blonde hair and brown doe eyes. She had a smile that went right through him.

"Hello, sir. I'm Candish."

"Hello Candish, I'm Bart. It is so nice to meet you." Bart said with a huge smile. He helped her out of the carriage.

Artis and Rachel stepped up to greet Randy and Candish, and then Bart and Artis removed their belongings from the carriage. Artis paid the carriage driver and asked Bart to load the belongings into his carriage.

"They are going to be living in the house we had set up for them. But I want all of us to eat lunch here at the restaurant before we go over there."

Bart smiled and said, "Sounds good boss. Miss Candish, I hope you are hungry. They have great food here."

Candish said, "Yes, Randy and I both were so nervous we didn't eat much breakfast. A good meal sounds wonderful."

Rachel whisked her away and Randy, Artis, and Bart worked on putting the belongings on the carriage.

"Randy, do you like to ride horses?" Bart asked him.

His little face lit up as he said, "Yes sir, but sometimes im scared cuz they are so big. They are Bigger'um me. One day, I be big too...youll see."

Artis and Bart smiled because they both knew a pony was waiting on him at his new house.

After the carriage was loaded, they went inside to join the women to eat lunch.

Rachel and Lilly Belle could tell instantly that Bart and Candish had instant chemistry. After lunch, they all gathered at Candish and Randy's new home to help unpack and get them settled in. Candish cried when she saw the house. It was adorable. A big porch, a living room, two big bedrooms, Randy's room had toys, and a beautiful kitchen, it was a dream come true. Randy was over the moon about his pony.

"I still have to run you a clothes line, but I will do that this week." Bart offered.

Candish said, "Thank you all so much. Our life has changed so much."

Artis suggested to Bart that once Candish had settled in after a couple of months she might become his bookkeeper if he thought she was able to handle the position. Bart thought that was a great idea. Although Bart was an adept bookkeeper that would free him up for other things he needed to attend to. Bookkeeping wasn't hard, but it was something that had to be done every day or you would fall behind. It gave Bart a good feeling of relief to know he would be getting some help.

Artis had already built a church and a schoolhouse in the community. The residents were using them faithfully. The women hung the unpacked Randy and Candish's clothes and personal belongings, and the men worked with Randy and his pony and helped set up the barn. They showed Randy how to feed and water his pony. They knew it would be a few years before he was doing it all by himself. Randy was so excited. Bart promised him he would be there to help him every day to take care of him.

A rider came rushing to them and screamed for Artis to come quickly.

"Sir there is an emergency. There has been a shooting at Kitty's. 2 men have shot Luther and McDonald at the door, and the bartender Mac."

McDonald and Luther were the men standing security and Mac was the stand-in bartender that Artis was trying out for the manager's spot.

Artis, Bart, and John Robert told the women to stay put and they rode out fast toward the town. They picked up 6 men in the community to ride with them as they entered the town. The shooters had taken all the women hostage and were threatening to kill them if Artis did not turn himself over to them.

Rett Henderson, the Marshall met them as they came into town. "Artis, you can't go in there you will be committing suicide. You can't do that to your daughter and your soon-to-be missus."

"How many are there? And why do they want me?" he asked.

"We think there are 3 of them. And they said you had their old brother Rasmus killed. They want revenge."

Artis said, "That's crazy. That idiot left on his own. We never saw him again after he nearly killed one of our girls."

Marshall Denby described what the men looked like so everyone would know they were the bad guys.

"We can't go in with guns a blazing because my girls will get hurt," Artis said. He was trying to think of a way to handle this so that no one got hurt.

The Marshall said, "Why don't I tell them I have you under arrest, and that I am turning you over to them? When they come out to get you... we handle our business."

Artis said, "If they are as stupid as their brother, they might fall for it."

John Robert and the Marshall had men in the front of the saloon near the

entranceway, and Bart and Artis had men in the back near the kitchen entranceway.

The restaurant had been evacuated. Mr. Smythe had a gun. He was on the floor

ready to fire when given instructions. He motioned that he had one of the shooters

in his sight. Then he held up 3 fingers showing there were 3 more, one behind the women, one at the front door to the right, and one on the staircase.

The Marshall called out to the outlaws, "Listen, boys, the word I got from the

owner of this establishment is that your brother went to North Carolina. He won a

bunch of land titles in a dice game and went to stake his claim there.

He was told there weren't any gold or silver mines there, just hundreds of acres of

land there. He was a happy man when he left out of here. So why in the world you

come here killing folks? This ain't right."

One of the brothers spit on the floor and called out, "Bull shit. Rasmus can't

read, and he damn sure can't play no cards."

The Marshall said, "Now before you go calling me a damn liar. I aint said nothing

bout no cards. They was having some big-time dice games, and he won every time

he threw the damn things. The owner, here, made them go outside to play cause he

don't allow no big gambling games in here. Your brother was sweeping the game

and winning every time he flung those dice. Folks are still talking about it. He hit

gold without ever touching another gold mine. That much land is extremely

valuable. Your brother is a very wealthy man today."

Another brother spoke up, "Well if that is so, why didn't he come get us?"

The Marshall said, "He was probably hightailing it out of here to go secure his

good fortune. If you don't claim your stake some folks will just plop right down on

it and steal it from under you. I would have done the same thing if I was him. Yall

ain't going no wheres, are you? Not planning on moving, eh? He will know how to find you."

"Well, we heard this is the last place he was seen, that's why we come up in here

to find out. The 2 guys at the door started talking trash, we shot them, then the

bartender reached for a shotgun and Davy shot him... it just sort of went bad fast.

We didn't mean to kill them; it just went bad quick. We decided to hold the girls

until the owner come talk to us." The brother on the steps called out.

The Marshall chuckled and said, "Look guys, for future reference, you can't go

around killing folks for talking trash. Most of this town would be hanging from

trees if that was the case. Let's just calm down and talk like men. Yall let them

girls go and come on and let's go find the owner and talk about this. He will tell

you the same thing I just told you. He will want to reopen this business and make

some money for himself. The girls need to get to work too."

"What about these folks we done shot?" Another brother asked.

"Well son, truth be told, some folks just need killing. We will get this worked out. I

know you all were concerned about your brother. I can understand the

misunderstanding."

The 4 brothers slowly came out to meet with the Marshall, they shook hands.

Artis, John Robert, and Bart came out and shot the brothers dead in the street.

Bart said, "Like you said Marshall, some folks just need killing."

———————————————————

It took a couple of hours to get things cleaned up and back to normal. Luther,
McDonald and Mac were carried over to the doctor's office where they would lie
in wait until coffins could be constructed for them. The outlaws were ironically
taken to the outskirts of town and buried in unmarked graves, just like their good-
for-nothing brother Rasmus. Perhaps he would explain all that when they had
their reunion in hell.
Artis didn't want to open up the saloon but his customers needed somewhere to
grieve. Luther and McDonald were their friends and they were hurting. He sent
Bart to get Lilly Belle and Rachel and bring them into town, and then Bart went
back to stay with Candish and Randy.
Lilly Belle cried over the loss of Luther and McDonald. They were good men and
had always treated her with such kindness and respect. She sobbed into John
Roberts arms. John Robert took her up to her room. He asked the doctor to come
and check on her. The doctor gave her a mild sedative. She never admitted to him
that she had orchestrated Rasmus's demise in a roundabout way, causing all of this
chaos and the murder of 3 men. She had not told anyone.
John Robert held her and whispered, "Whatever happened to Rasmus and his

brothers was their own fault. They were terrible no-gooders, honey. They all asked

for what they received. Unfortunately, sometimes good people suffer at the hands

of miserable scum.

All we can do is survive Lilly Belle and get our revenge by living a good life.

Something most no-gooders will never do because they are so busy trying to ruin

things for everyone else. Jesus died for all of us, but not everyone receives him.

The no-gooders reject him and nothing good comes of them."

Lilly Belle looked at him and smiled, "Yes, my love. I agree with you. Their kind

reject anything good."

Artis came in and hugged her. "I'm so thankful this is over. I just hope they don't have any more brothers."

The three of them laughed and agreed with Artis.

Lilly Belle said, "Dad, I must get up and send a wire to Mac's family about his death."

Artis said, "Sweetheart, Mac did not have any family. None at all. That is why we

are paying for his burial. You rest. The doctor said you are in shock but rest will

cause it to go away. All of the girls are fine. The customers insisted we open Kitty's

tonight so they could grieve the loss of their friends and check on the girls. Honey,

you would have been so proud of Mr. Smythe hunkered down with a gun, on the

floor, ready to defend us. He is definitely getting a raise."

He and John Robert laughed and Lilly Belle snored. The sedative had kicked in

and she was sound asleep. John Robert covered her up and the two men went

downstairs. Marshall Denby was waiting on them at the bar.

"First rounds on me guys." The Marshall called out, raising his mug.

One of the working girls had gotten behind the bar and was in the position of the

bartender. Her name was Tricia. She pulled two more drafts and presented them to

Artis and John Robert.

They all three raised their mugs, John Robert toasted, "Here is to law and order,

every time."

The men touched their mugs and then drank a long drink of their beers.

After having several rounds Artis went to Mr. Smythe and told him how much he

appreciated his assistance earlier in the day.

"It's no problem, sir. Lilly Belle always say, we are family. A man protects his

family." Mr. Smythe said with a grin. He was a huge, humble man with a good

heart. Artis knew he was lucky to have him.

"Do you mind I ask if Miss Lilly Belle okay? I saw her upset and I saw doctor."

"The doctor said she has what is called shock, meaning she is very upset about

those killed here this afternoon. She just needs rest. He gave her something to

sleep. He says she will be okay. I will tell her you asked."

Mr. Smythe shook his head yes and said, "Hmm I pray. I know she be okay. She is

good lady. God protect her."

"Oh by the way, one of the girls is being the bartender tonight so she is not getting

her usual pay from upstairs. Do you have something the drinkers could maybe put

tips in on the bar for her?" Artis asked.

Mr. Smythe smiled and said, "Yes sir."

He went to the storage room and brought back 7 blue Ball glass jars.

"Put them around bar. They will fill up. You see."

"Mr. Smythe you are a genius."

Artis took them to the bar and placed them around the bar. He put money in each

jar and told the patrons, "Don't forget to tip your bartender men. She's losing

money by serving you down here instead of upstairs tonight."

Artis taught Tricia how to write down which girl took a date upstairs and how to

claim the money. He taught her to have the girl sign the receipt so there was proof

the man had paid. Tricia knew how it worked because she too was a working girl

but she didn't know how to document it like she was learning now. At the end of

the night, the girls should tip her from the tips they received from their dates.

Tricia was very surprised at how much she made from the bar tips. She emptied the

jars several times during the night and put them back on the bar. When they closed, she asked Artis if he would consider allowing her to work as the bartender.

"Are you tired of working upstairs Tricia? He asked her.

"Yes and No sir. I'm getting older. I want a change. Tonight, with the customers,

they didn't get to pick me, I had a say, and I didn't have to sleep with nobody. I can

just take my earnings and go to sleep. I feel different.

Maybe if you let me do this, I can save my money and buy one of your houses and

start a garden my whole life can change. I always wanted to raise chickens, and

maybe rabbits. I used to be good with plants."

Artis sighed and said, "Okay listen. This is going to mean I have to trust you

completely. You will be handling my money. If I can't trust you, there is no sense in us doing this.

I will talk to Lilly Belle. She has the final say. We can train you. We have been

looking for managers for the bar and the restaurant. There is a lot more to it than

slinging drinks and flirting. You have to be good with getting the money. You also

have to know when a man has had enough and not sell him anymore to drink. That

is when you get the security guys to come sit at the bar next to him. They will tell him it's time to go."

Tricia said, "So far, I understand what you are saying. I had fun tonight even with the day starting so bad, the night ended up good."

Artis smiled and said, "Yes it did."

John Robert and Marshall Denby also stayed until closing just to make sure there was no more trouble. John Robert went up to check on Lilly Belle but she was still

sleeping. He asked Artis if he could sleep on the floor next to her bed. Artis agreed.

They just wanted her to feel safe when she woke up. Artis went over to the Hotel

and slept on Rachel's sofa.

Bart and Candish had a long talk after Randy had gone to bed. They drank coffee

over an open fire pit and looked at the stars. Candish shared her story and Bart

shared his. They became friends quickly, both realizing they had so much in

common, both realizing they would be good for each other. They laughed,

and shared good stories about their lives, and painful ones. When it was time for

Bart to go, he reassured her that Moosehead was a good town and that things did

not ordinarily happen like the shooting and apologized she and Randy moved here

just when something like that happened.

Candish said, "You don't have to apologize for something other folks did Bart. I

appreciate you trying to comfort me. I know how the world is, there are always

going to be bad people."

Bart smiled at her. "Candish, I have something to give you. You have to keep it

away from Randy, it is strictly for your protection when I am not around, okay?"

Candish shakes her head, yes, and Bart hands her a small 5-shot revolver. It was
small enough to fit in her purse. "When you get settled in, we will do some
practice shooting so you will be confident if you ever have to use it. But please
never let Randy know where you keep it. Guns can be considered toys by children.
I have seen too many children killed by thinking guns were toys and shooting
themselves or someone else."

Candish hugged Bart and said, "I swear, I will be extra careful Bart. Thank you for thinking of our safety. Now come back in the morning and eat breakfast with us."

Bart chuckled and said, "I will be honored to ma'am." He tipped his hat as he rode away.

Bart was on cloud 9 on the ride to his house. It wasn't very far but he found
himself thanking God. "Sir, I can't believe I am feeling love again. She's perfect.
She's beautiful and funny, her eyes light up when she sees me. She wanted to know

about me, not just talk about herself. She loves her baby brother so much and he is

a great kid. I mean, she is everything I could ask you for. I never really thought I

would feel this way again. Oh, and sir, she loves horses and she can cook."

Bart blushed a little bit, "I know that you know all this already, and I know that

nobody is perfect but you God, I just meant, she is perfect for me. Please show me

how to be the right man for her God. Thank you for listening God. I'm signing off

now."

Bart pulled onto his property and headed to the barn to put up his horse and take care of all the other horses. He slept better that night than he had in years.

Seven months went by. Tricia was a magnificent bartender. She worked so hard

that her time working in the upstairs was over. Artis officially named her the bar

manager. She hired 2 more bartenders and arranged a schedule where they all 3

would rotate the schedules and it would not work just one bartender to death. On

days they didn't work the bar, they could help in the restaurant to earn extra

money.

Rachel and Lilly Belle were busy planning their weddings. They had most of

everything worked out except where they were going to have it. Lilly Belle, Rachel and Artis had approached the Reverend Bronson of the local church however, he

said, "I just don't feel like it's proper with you two owning a saloon, for me to

conduct your matrimonial ceremonies."

Rachel was hurt and said, "You know Reverend, you sure don't mind accepting our

donations of money, clothing, and food that we give to the church every single

month for the poor. Not to mention the free services my fiancé and other men

provide to the church when something needs repair."

He stuttered, "Well that is different, that is for the underprivileged."

Rachel stood up and said, "If you do not perform our weddings, we will stop

contributing our donations and we will tell the people they should ask for an in-

depth investigation as to where their financial donations are being used. You and

your very young missus seem to live in a very high and mighty lifestyle. Extra nice

home, expensive carriages, expensive clothing, servants in the home. Yes, I think

an audit should be called for by the people."

The reverend turned white and said, "You are blackmailing me!"

Lilly Belle spoke up and said, "No, she is calling you out on your hypocrisy." then

she motioned for Rachel and Artis to follow her and leave.

They went back to Kitty's to have lunch. Rachel was still mad and said, "Listen,

Artis, even if that phony comes crawling in here on his knees, I don't want him to perform our ceremony. We will find someone else. Maybe Lilly Belle could

advertise for a Pastor to come here from another city."

Artis kissed her hand and said, "That is a great idea sweetheart. Lilly Belle?"

Lilly Belle smiled and said, "Yes, I will be happy to do that. Rachel let's work on

what we want it to say after lunch."

Rachel agreed.

John Robert joined them. He had been at the site of the new house being built. It

was coming along great. His timing was perfect to hear all about their morning.

Bart, Candish, and Randy came riding up and joined them for lunch.

"We have an announcement to make," Bart said with a smile.

Candish held out her hand and showed her engagement ring. "We are getting

married!"

Everyone at the table cheered! They all hugged Bart and Candish.

Randy was giggling. "I'm getting a Daddy." He kept telling everyone.

Artis mussed his hair and said, "Yes you are Randy, and a great one at that."

After the excitement calmed down, Rachel and Lilly Belle explained the fight with

the Reverend earlier. Candish looked concerned, but they assured her they would

find a pastor to marry all 3 of them.

After lunch, Bart and John Robert took Randy over to the Hardware store to buy a

few things. Artis went into the Saloon to count last night's money and to open up

for business. The place looked great.

Tricia had hired someone to clean at closing time and the man did a fine job. All

the tables were scrubbed down, the floors swept. He even wiped down the walls.

Her deal with him was he had to show her everything he found on the floor, and

she decided if he could keep it all or split it with her. He was satisfied with that. In

return, he received one meal a day and $2.00 a day. He was well worth it because

he did a great job. His name was Earl Barker.

While the men were gone, the women sat around a table with a pencil and paper to write the advertisement for a pastor.

"In search of a Christian Pastor to perform the wedding ceremonies for 3 Brides and 3 Grooms. The ceremony of all 3 will happen at the same time to conserve time and energy. The ceremonies will be outside so that all of their friends and family can attend. Please send your credentials and fee request to P.O. Box 1912 Moosehead, California, in the care of Lilly Belle. Please send references. Do not show up until we send for you. If we do accept you to perform the service, all of your expenses will be paid. (transportation to and from, Hotel stay up to 3 nights, meals at the hotel, and needs from the hotel store)

This is Time Sensitive. Please answer promptly"

The women read and reread the advertisement. It sounded good to all of them.

They walked it over to the Post Office, where Mr. Byrd made a large copy for them

for the side of the carriage.

He also made 10 copies for the churches in nearby towns and addressed them to be sent out with the next carriage.

"Well, ladies. We need to make sure everything is ready for when a pastor agrees

to do the services. Candish get Bart into a suit. Hopefully, all the guys can wear

nice grey suits, if that is okay with you girls?" Rachel said with a grin.

They both said yes!

"And Candish, yall come over to the Hotel. I bought 2 wedding dresses. One is too

small and I believe it will fit you perfectly. Come see if you like it."

They walked over to the hotel.

The dress was gorgeous and yes it fit beautifully. Candish cried.

Candish in her beautiful wedding dress.

The men and Randy came back from the Hardware store. Candish and Bart took

Randy home. Candish broke the news to Bart that their engagement would be short

and he was thrilled.

"That is fine by me Candish. I wish we could be married right now."

"I got my wedding dress today, so as soon as a minister answers Lilly Belle's

advertisement the ball will start rolling. I need to get you back into town to get a

suit. If there is one you can already fit into that will be fine but it needs to be grey.

Just tell the salesman, he will understand." She said with a smile.

Bart laughed and said, "Yes ma'am."

"We are all getting married at the same time, all of you guys will be married in grey suits and us girls will have different gowns. I'm so excited for this. I don't have many friends as you know, so this is exciting for me." Candish gushed.

Bart hugged her and said, "Darlin' I won't see anyone but you."

He left her and Randy to go into town to look for his suit. He ran into John Robert, who was looking upset.

"What's wrong buddy? You are looking worried." Bart asked.

"Well, there are not any grey suits here in Moosehead. We are going to have to get our measurements here, the shop owner will send them ahead to Agora, and in 3 days we can go pick up the suits. Me and Artis already got measured so it's your turn. I just don't like the idea of leaving our families to go pick up those suits."

Bart thought out loud, "Why don't you just tell them we will pay extra to have them brought here to us?"

John Robert's face lit up. "Man, I didn't think of that!" he ran fast back into the shop where they measured him, then came out smiling,

"They agreed! Now come on in here and get measured. I guess my nerves just got the best of me."

They had a good laugh. Artis came in and said he had just sent a post requesting 3 bouquets for the brides and 3 flowers for their suits.

"The postmaster called them boutonnieres. Apparently, we pin them to our suits. Mr. Smythe is cooking lunch for us and any visitors that show up but Lilly Belle got a message from the Women's Auxiliary of the local church that refused to marry us, that they are serving food also for I think it's called the perception or reception. Our women decided we are not serving alcohol at the wedding or reception since the nice ladies from the church were sending food. Rachel said it's about respect."

John Robert and Bart said they agreed, then they all chuckled.

Four days later, the 3 grey suits arrived and they fit perfectly, as did the shoes. Artis

had ordered 50 benches and had a huge arch made for the brides and grooms to

stand in front of when they said their vows.

The 3 brides to be received 20 answers to their advertisements. They called for 3 to

be interviewed. Out of the 3 they chose, Pastor Raymond Thunder. He was a nice

older man. He and his wife Bernadette came from Alabama to take over a

small church in Agora. He was very personable and was not judgmental.

He was eager to perform the ceremony. His only request was that everyone believe

in God. He spoke to each couple independently and was satisfied.

The weddings were scheduled to take place in 2 days. Everyone worked feverishly

to get the area ready for the big event.

The saloon was closed on Saturday and everyone who was friends or family of the

brides and grooms attended the weddings at 11:00 am. Pastor Thunder performed

an amazing ceremony. 5-year-old Randy was everyone's best man and escorted

each bride down the aisle.

Between Mr. Smythe and the Women's Auxiliary, there was so much food. It was

serviced picnic style. There were also 3 wedding cakes for the married couples to

cut. Everyone had a wonderful time and everyone behaved like perfect ladies and

gentlemen.

The day was like a fairy tale for all 3 of the couples. John Robert paid a couple of

men; to play fiddles and guitars so people could dance under a makeshift tent. The

party lasted until about 8 pm.

Mr. Smythe supervised the maintenance crew, that dismantled the event items and

Artis had given him the money to square up with everyone from the preacher to the

band.

Afterward, Mr. Smythe went back to Kitties and opened the restaurant for business.

Several of the working girls helped him by waiting tables and collecting the money

for the meals. They did not work upstairs that night. They felt like proper ladies

after being present at a real wedding.

Security was not lazy on the door that night. They prevented 7 unruly, drunk men

from entering the restaurant. The men were demanding the saloon be opened up,

one began firing his gun in the air in protest. Kitty's security tackled the drunk men

and took their knives and guns, drug them each around to the side of the building,

and sent someone for the sheriff who locked them all up. They were so drunk it

took 3 days for them to sober up.

Security handled it very well. Mr. Smythe came out and told everyone they were

getting a discount on their meals for the inconvenience and he apologized. The

restaurant guests clapped for him. The restaurant remained open until 10:00 pm

and then closed for the night in celebration of the weddings. Security decided to

sleep in the saloon to make sure there were no more disturbances, Mr. Smythe slept

in his room near the kitchen and the working girls slept upstairs in their rooms. It

was a peaceful night.

Photographs from the wedding.

Rachel Lilly Belle Cardis

Artis sold Kitty's for a large amount of money, to a decent friend of his. The new owner Frank Ezer, kept all of the employees of the saloon. Artis shared the money with his daughter, Lilly Belle.

He sold the restaurant separately to Mr. Smythe, who was so happy to own it. He then ran his real estate business with Bart and enjoyed it. His wife Rachel had 3 children.

Bart continued to work for Artis for many years. His bride gave him 5 more children and Randy worked with his father as he grew up. Bart opened a hardware store and it was successful.

John Robert and Lilly Belle had 2 children. They built a huge farm. They bought and sold livestock. It was a lucrative business.

The End (for now)

Also by Lilly Buchanan

Bad girls
Jezebel
Rahab

King Marc 1
King Marc

Life in a small town
New Life in a Small Town

Standalone
Our Second Chance
Dannie
Leroy
Sugah
The Wright House
Jezebel 2
Kitty's

About the Author

Lilly Buchanan is originally from Columbus, Georgia. She currently lives in Pascagoula, Mississippi. Lilly started writing when she was a little girl. Lilly loves pretty things, flowers, decorating, writing beautiful stories, volunteering and Jesus! Lilly has 2 amazing granddaughters, Jasmine and Alexandria. If you stop and ask she will show you pictures!!

About the Publisher

Self publishing with Draft to Digital has been an amazing experience.